Dear Parent:
Your child's love of reading starts here

Every child learns to read in a different way and at his or her own speed. You can help your young reader improve and become more confident by encouraging his or her own interests and abilities. You can also guide your child's spiritual development by reading stories with biblical values and Bible stories, like I Can Read! books published by Zonderkidz. From books your child reads with you to the first books he or she reads alone, there are I Can Read! books for every stage of reading:

SHARED READING
Basic language, word repetition, and whimsical illustrations, ideal for sharing with your emergent reader.

BEGINNING READING
Short sentences, familiar words, and simple concepts for children eager to read on their own.

READING WITH HELP
Engaging stories, longer sentences, and language play for developing readers.

READING ALONE
Complex plots, challenging vocabulary, and high-interest topics for the independent reader.

ADVANCED READING
Short paragraphs, chapters, and exciting themes for the perfect bridge to chapter books.

I Can Read! books have introduced children to the joy of reading since 1957. Featuring award-winning authors and illustrators and a fabulous cast of beloved characters, I Can Read! books set the standard for beginning readers.

A lifetime of discovery begins with the magical words **"I Can Read!"**

Visit www.icanread.com for information on enriching your child's reading experience.
Visit www.zonderkidz.com for more Zonderkidz I Can Read! titles.

Do not be wise in your own eyes;

fear the Lord and shun evil.

This will bring health to your body

and nourishment to your bones.

—*Proverbs 3:7-8*

ZONDERKIDZ

The Berenstain Bears® Thank God for Good Health
Copyright© 2013 by Berenstain Publishing, Inc.
Illustrations © 2013 by Berenstain Publishing, Inc.

Requests for information should be addressed to:

Zondervan, 5300 Patterson Ave SE, Grand Rapids, Michigan 49530

Library of Congress Cataloging-in-Publication Data

Berenstain, Stan, 1923-2005
   [Berenstain bears go to the doctor]
   The Berenstain bears thank God for good health / Stan and Jan
Berenstain with Mike Berenstain.
      p. cm. — (I can read) (Living Lights)
     Summary: Dr. Grizzly gives the Berenstain cubs a regular checkup.
   ISBN 978-0-310-72503-9
   [1. Medical care—Fiction 2. Bears—Fiction. 3. Christian life—Fiction.]
  I. Berenstain, Jan, 1923-2012. II. Berenstain, Mike, 1951- III. Title.
  PZ7.B4483Bfg 2013
  E—dc23   2012030233

Editor: Mary Hassinger
Design: Diane Mielke

Printed in China

12 13 14 15 16 17 /DSC/ 10 9 8 7 6 5 4 3 2 1

The Berenstain Bears
Thank God for Good Health

Story and Pictures By
Stan & Jan Berenstain with Mike Berenstain

 Living Lights

ZONDERVAN.com/
AUTHORTRACKER
follow your favorite authors

"The doctor?" said Brother and Sister.
"Why?"

"It is time for a check-up,"
said Mama.

"A check-up?"
said Brother.
"Phooey!"

"A check-up helps make sure
you stay well," said Mama.
Then she put on her hat.

"Papa and I pray to God for good health every day," said Mama. "Now, come along."

"Mama? Papa? Will Dr. Grizzly

give us a shot?" Brother asked.

Mama said, "Maybe a booster shot."

"Stop!" said Sister when they were
on their way. "This is the wrong road."
Papa said, "This is the right road."

"Turn back!" said Brother.

"I saw a lost dog."

Papa said, "There was no lost dog."

The Bears got to

Dr. Grizzly's office.

"What a crowd," said Brother.

"We will be here all day."

"Patience is a virtue," said Mama. "The Good Book says, 'A person's wisdom yields patience.'"

It was Brother and Sister's turn.
"Hello," said Dr. Gert Grizzly.
"It's time for your
check-ups."

"Hop up, Sister.
It is your turn first,"
said Dr. Grizzly.

"Let me check your tummy," she said.

"Please tell me if it hurts."

"Well," said Dr. Grizzly.

"What do you say?"

"No problem," said Sister.

"Very good," said the doctor.

"What is that?" asked Brother.

Brother was pointing at

something the doctor was holding.

"It is one of my tools.

It is a stethoscope.

It lets me listen to

your heart,"

said the doctor.

"Now for your ears," said Dr. Grizzly.

"I hope they are clean,"
said Sister.

"Just fine!

Now tell me what you hear

when I whisper,"

said the doctor.

"You said, 'So far, so good,'" said the cubs.

"Hear that, Mama?" asked Papa. "God has blessed our cubs with good health."

"Now your eyes," said Dr. Grizzly.

"Please read the small letters."

"A, P, R, I, O, U, Z," said both cubs.

"Very good! The Bible says,

'If your eyes are healthy,

your whole body will be full of light.'"

"Next, step on the scale,"
said the doctor.

"We will check your weight."

"Thirty-seven for Sister and forty-six for Brother.

"I am proud of you both," said Dr. Grizzly. "You have taken good care of your bodies. God has blessed you with good health."

Papa said, "Those cubs
are just like old Papa Q. Bear—
very healthy!

Now … may I get weighed?"
"Of course," said Dr. Grizzly.

The doctor looked at the scale.
"Well, Papa," said the doctor,
"God is looking after the cubs but
you need to start looking after you!"

"Thank you, Dr. Grizzly,"

said Brother and Sister.

"So long!"

"Wait just a minute. I almost forgot.
You both need a booster shot,"
said the doctor.

"But," said Sister,
"if we are healthy, why do
we need a shot?"

"This special shot keeps you healthy,"
Dr. Grizzly said.

Sister was first.

"This may hurt for half a minute,"

said the doctor.

But it was not bad!

"Are you brave like Sister?"

Dr. Grizzly asked Brother.

And he was.

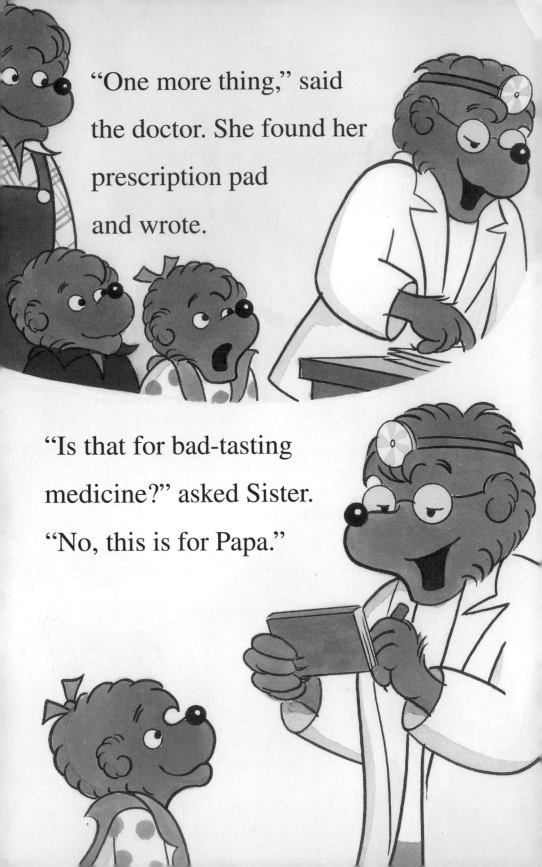

"One more thing," said the doctor. She found her prescription pad and wrote.

"Is that for bad-tasting medicine?" asked Sister. "No, this is for Papa."

"Here, Papa," said the doctor.

"Follow these directions."

Rₓ Papa Bear:
No dessert until
you lose ten pounds.

"But, Doc," said Papa,

as he read the note. "I will starve."

"Now, now," Dr. Grizzly said.

"See you in

six months."

"Carrot sticks, anyone?"

Papa asked at dessert that day.

"No thanks," said Brother.

"Well, Lord," said Papa.

"We give thanks for all your blessings—
including carrot sticks!"